William Schwenck Gilbert

Pygmalion and Galatea

An Original Mythological Comedy

William Schwenck Gilbert

Pygmalion and Galatea
An Original Mythological Comedy

ISBN/EAN: 9783337021801

Printed in Europe, USA, Canada, Australia, Japan

Cover: Foto ©Andreas Hilbeck / pixelio.de

More available books at **www.hansebooks.com**

PYGMALION AND GALATEA.

AN ORIGINAL

MYTHOLOGICAL COMEDY.

IN THREE ACTS.

BY W. S. GILBERT.

DRAMATIC ▐▇▇▇▇▇▇ COMPANY.

PYGMALION AND GAL█████

DRAMATIS PERSONÆ.

	Original, Haymarket, London, Dec. 9th, 1871.	Lyceum, London, Dec. 8th, 1883.
PYGMALION (*an Athenian sculptor*).	Mr. W. H. Kendal.	Mr. J. H. Barnes.
LEUCIPPE (*a soldier*)	Mr. Howe.	Mr. F. H. Macklin.
CHRYSOS (*an art patron*)	Mr. J. B. Buckstone.	Mr. H. Kemble.
AGESIMOS (*Chrysos' slave*)	Mr. Braid.	Mr. E. T. March.
MINOS (*Pygmalion's slave*)	Mr. Weathersby.	Mr. Arthur Lewis.
GALATEA (*an animated statue*)	Miss M. Robertson.	Miss Mary Anderson.
CYNISCA (*Pygmalion's wife*)	Miss Caroline Hill.	Miss Amy Roselle.
DAPHNE (*Chrysos' wife*)	Mrs. Chippendale.	Mrs. Arthur Stirling.
MYRINE (*Pygmalion's sister*)	Miss Merton.	Miss Annie Rose.

SCENE: PYGMALION'S STUDIO.

[*The action is comprised within the space of twenty-four hours.
Time occupied in representation, one hour and three-quarters.*]

NOTE.—The statue of Galatea should be modelled expressly to resemble the lady who plays the part. If this is impracticable, some existing statue may be used, but it is essential that its drapery should be perfectly modest and simple. The "change" from the statue to the living person is most conveniently effected by means of a properly counter weighted "turn-table," on which the actress and statue are placed back to back, with what is technically known as a "backing" between them. The two curtains that conceal the statute should "travel" on two separate but parallel iron rods, three inches apart, and the curtains should be broad enough to *overlap* each other three or four inches.

STAGE DIRECTIONS.

R. means Riget of Stage, facing the Audience; L. Left; C. Centre; R. C. Right of Centre; L. C. Left of Centre. D. F. Door in the Flat, or Scene running across the back of the Stage; C. D. F. Centre Door in the Flat; R. D. F. Right Door in the Flat; L. C. F. Left Door in the Flat; R. D. Right Door: L. D. Left Door; 1 E. First Entrance; 2 E. Second Entrance; U. E. Upper Entrance; 1, 2 or 3 G. First, Second or Third Groove.

R.	R. C.	C.	L. C.	L.

The Reader is supposed to be on the Stage, facing the Audience.

PYGMALION AND GALATEA.

ACT I.

SCENE: PYGMALION'S STUDIO.

[*Several classical statues are placed about the room; at the back a temple or cabinet containing a statue of* GALATEA, *before which curtains are drawn concealing the statue from the audience. The curtains must be so contrived that they will open readily and display the statue completely, without much effort on the part of the actor who opens them. They must also be fitted with mechanical appliances to close apparently of their own accord at the latter part of Act III.; doors,* R. *and* L., I. E. L. 3rd E., *and opening* U. E. R.]

[MIMOS, *a slave, is discovered at work,* L. C., *on a half finished statue. To him enter* AGESIMOS, U. E. R.; *he is magnificently dressed; he comes down* R. C.]

AGES. (*haughtily.*) Good day. Is this Pygmalion's studio?
MIM. (*bowing.*) It is.
AGES. Are you Pygmalion?
MIM. Oh, no;
I am his slave.
AGES. And has Pygmalion slaves?
A sculptor with a slave to wait on him;
A slave to fetch and carry—come and go—
And p'raps a whip to thrash him if he don't!
What's the world coming to? (*sits* R. C.)
MIM. What is your will?
AGES. This: Chrysos will receive Pygmalion
At half-past three to-day; so bid him come.
MIM. And are you Chrysos, sir?

AGES.   Well, no I'm not.
That is, not altogether, I'm in fact,
His slave.

MIM. (*relieved*.) His slave! ha, ha!

AGES. (*very proudly — rises*)—   My name's Agesimos!

MIM. And has Agesimos a master then,
To bid him fetch and carry—come and go—
And wield a whip to thrash him if he don't?
What's the world coming to? (*Resumes work.*)

AGES.   Poor purblind fool!
I'd sooner tie the sandals of my lord,
Than own five hundred thousand such as you.
Whip! why Agesimos would rather far
Be whipped by Chrysos seven times a day,
Than whip you hence to the Acropolis;
What say you now?

MIM.   Why, that upon one point
Agesimos and I are quite agreed.
And who is Chrysos?

AGES.   Hear the slave, ye gods,
He knows not Chrysos.

MIM.   Verily, not I.

AGES. He is the chiefest man in Athens, sir;
The father of the arts—a nobleman
Of princely liberality and taste,
On whom five hundred starved Pygmalions
May batten if they will.

Enter PYGMALION, U. E. R., *down* C.

PYG.   Who is this man?   [Agesimos.

AGES. (*humbly*) I'm Chrysos' slave—(*proudly*) my name's
Chrysos has heard of you; he understands
That you have talent, and he condescends
To bid you call on him. But take good care
How you offend him; he can make or mar!

PYG. Your master's slave reflects his insolence!
Tell him from me that, though I'm poor enough,
I am an artist and a gentleman.
He should not reckon Art among his slaves;
She rules the world—so let him wait on her.

AGES. This is a sculptor!

PYG. (*furiously*)—   And an angry one!
Begone, and take my message to your lord.
                    [*Exit* AGESIMOS, R. U. E.
Insolent hound!

Enter CYNISCA, R. I. E.

CYN.   Pygmalion, what's amiss?
PYG. Chrysos has sent his slave to render me
The customary tribute paid by wealth
To mere intelligence.
CYN.   Pygmalion!
Brooding upon the chartered insolence
Of a mere slave!   Dismiss the thought at once.
Come, take thy chisel, thou hast work to do
Ere thy wife-model takes her leave to-day;
In half-an-hour I must be on the road
To Athens.   Half-an-hour remains to thee—
Come—make the most of it—I'll pose myself;
Say—will that do?   (*Poses herself against base* R.)
PYG.   I cannot work to-day.
My hand's uncertain—I must rest awhile.
CYN. Then rest and gaze upon thy masterpiece,
'Twill reconcile thee to thyself—Behold!

(*Draws curtain and discovers statue of* GALATEA.*

PYG. Yes—for in gazing on my handiwork,
I gaze on heaven's handiwork—thyself—
CYN. And yet, although it be thy masterpiece,
It has the fault thy patrons find with all
Thy many statues.
PYG.   What then do they say?
CYN. They say Pygmalion's statues have one head—
That head, Cynisca's.
PYG.   So, then, it's a fault (*rises*)
To reproduce an hundred thousand fold,
For the advantage of mankind at large,   [*hand.*)
The happiness the gods have given me! (*Takes her*
Well, when I find a fairer head than thine
I'll give my patrons some variety.

* NOTE.—These curtains must be pushed aside by hand—not
drawn apart by arrangement of cord and pulleys.

CYN. (*hastily.*)   I would not have thee find another head
That seemed as fair to thee for all the world!
We'll have no stranger models if you please,
I'll be your model, sir, as heretofore,
So reproduce me at your will; and yet
It were sheer vanity in me to think
That this fair stone recalls Cynisca's face.

PYG. Cynisca's face in every line!

CYN.   No, no!   [*up* L.)
Those outlines softened, angles smoothed away
The eyebrows arched, the head more truly poised,
The forehead ten years smoother than mine own,
Tell rather of Cynisca as she was
When, in the silent groves of Artemis,
Pygmalion told his love ten years ago;
And then the placid brow, the sweet, sad lips,
The gentle head down-bent resignedly,
Proclaim that this is not Pygmalion's wife, [tween!
Who laughs and frowns, but knows no meed be-
I am no longer as that statue is (*down* L.)   (*Closes*
                                                    [*curtains.*)

PYG. Why here's ingratitude, to slander Time,
Who in his hurried course has passed thee by!
Or is it that Cynisca won't allow
That Time *could* pass her by, and never pause
To print a kiss upon so fair a face?

Enter MYRINE, R. U. E., *running.*

MYR. (*down* R. C.) Pygmalion I have news.

PYG. (C.)—   My sister, speak.

MYR. (*bashfully.*) Send Mimos hence.   [quite alone.

PYG. (*signs to* MIMOS, *who exits* L. *and* D.)   Now we are

MYR. Leucippe—

CYN. (L. C.)   Well!

MYR. (*to* PYG.)—   He was thy schoolfellow,
And thou and he are brothers save in blood;
He loves my brother as a brother.

PYG.   Yes,
I'm sure of that; but is that all thy news?
There's more to come!

MYR. (*bashfully.*)   He loves thy sister too.

PYG. Why this is news, Myrine—kiss me girl.

                 (*Kisses her and puts her to c.*)

I'm more than happy at thy happiness,
There is no better fellow in the world.

CYN. But tell us all about it dear. How came
The awkward, bashful, burly warrior,
To nerve himself to this confession?

       LEUCIPPE *appears at door* U. E. R.

MYR.   Why—
He's here—(*goes to him and brings him down*)—
and he shall tell thee how it was.

LEUC. (*awkwardly.*) In truth I hardly know, I'm new at it;
I'm but a soldier. Could I fight my way
Into a maiden's heart, why well and good;
I'd get there somehow. But to talk and sigh,
And whisper pretty things, I can't do that;
I tried it, but I stammered, blushed and failed.
Myrine laughed at me—but bless her heart,
She knew my meaning and she pulled me through!

MYR. I don't know how, Pygmalion, but I did.
He stammered, as he tells you, and I laughed;
And then I felt so sorry, when I saw
The great, big, brave Leucippe look so like
A beaten schoolboy—that I think I cried. (*Pause.*)
And then—I quite forgot what happened next.
Till, by some means, we, who had always been
So cold and formal, distant and polite,
Found ourselves——

LEUC.   Each upon the other's neck!
You are not angry? (*offering his hand.*)

PYG. (*taking it.*)   Angry? overjoyed!
I wish I had been there, unseen, to see;
No sight could give me greater happiness!

LEUC. What! say you so? Why then, Myrine, girl,
We'll reproduce it for his benefit. (*They embrace.*)
See here, Pygmalion, here's a group for thee!
Come, fetch thy clay, and set to work on it,
I'll promise thee thy models will not tire.

CYN. How now, Leucippe, where's the schoolboy blush,
That used to coat thy face at sight of her?

LEUC. The coating was but thin, we've rubbed it off!
            (*Kisses* MYRINE *and takes her to seat* L.)

PYG. Take care of him, Myrine; thou hast not
    The safeguard that protects *her*.
            (*Indicating* CYNISCA, *who crosses* R. C.)

MYR. (*sits* L.)—   What is that?

CYN. (*seated* R.)   It's a strange story.   Many years ago
    I was a holy nymph of Artemis,
    Pledged to eternal maidenhood.

LEUC.   Indeed!

MYR. How terrible!

CYN.   It seems not so to me;
    For weeks and weeks I pondered stedfastly
    Upon the nature of that serious step
    Before I took it—lay awake at night,
    Looking upon it from this point and that,
    And I at length determined that the vow,
    Which to Myrine seems so terrible,
    Was one that I, at all events could keep.
            (LEUCIPPE *whispers* MYRINE.)

MYR. How old was thou, Cynisca?

CYN.   I was ten.
    Well—in due course, I reached eleven, still
    I saw no reason to regret the step;   [changed;
    Twelve — thirteen — fourteen saw me still un-
    At fifteen, it occurred to me one day
    That marriage was a necessary ill,
    Inflicted by the gods to punish us,
    And to evade it were impiety;
    At sixteen the idea became more fixed;
    At seventeen I was convinced of it.

PYG. In the meantime she'd seen Pygmalion.
       (PYG. *is up* L. *working on unfinished statue.*)

MYR. And you confided all you doubts to him?

CYN. I did, and he endorsed them—so we laid
    The case before my mistress Artemis;
    No need to tell the arguments we used,
    Suffice it that they brought about our end.
    And Artemis, her icy steadfastness
    Thawed by the ardor of Cynisca's prayers,
    Replied, " Go girl, and wed Pygmalion;

"But mark my words—(*rises and crosses* c.)--
  whichever one of you,
"Or he or she, shall falsify the vow
"Of perfect conjugal fidelity—
"The wronged one, he or she, shall have the power
"To call down *blindness* on the backslider,
"And sightless shall the truant mate remain
"Until expressly pardoned by the other."

LEUC. It's fortunate such powers as your's are not
  In universal use; for if they were,
  One half the husbands and one half the wives
  Would be as blind as night; the other half,
  Having their eyes, would use them—on each other!

MIMOS *enters,* U. E. L., *and gives* PYGMALION *a scroll,
which he reads at back. Exit* MIMOS U. E. L.

MYR. But then, the power of calling down this doom
  Remains with thee. Thou wouldst not burden him
  With such a curse as utter sightlessness,
  However grieviously he might offend.

CYN. (*earnestly*). I love Pygmalion for his faithfulness;
  The act that robs him of that quality
  Will rob him of the love that springs from it.

MYR. But sightlessness—it is so terrible!

CYN. And faithfulness—it is so terrible!
  I take my temper from Pygmalion;
  While he is god-like—he's a god to me,
  And should he turn to devil, I'll turn with him,
  I know no half moods, I am love or hate!

MYR. (*to* LEUC.)—What do you say to that?

LEUC. Why, on the whole I'm glad *you're* not a nymph of
  Artemis!

[*Exeunt,* MYRINE *and* LEUCIPPE, I. E. L.

PYG. I've brought him to his senses. Presently
  My patron Chrysos will be here to earn
  Some thousand drachmas. (*Down* R.)

CYN. (L. C.)   How, my love, to earn?
  He is a man of unexampled wealth,
  And follows no profession.

PYG.   Yes, he does;

He is a patron of the Arts, and makes
A handsome income by his patronage.

CYN. How so?

PYG.   He is an ignorant buffoon!
But purses hold a higher rank than brains,
And he is rich; wherever Chrysos buys,
The world of smaller fools comes following,
And men are glad to sell their work to him
At half its proper price, that they my say,
" Chrysos has purchased handiwork of ours."
He is a fashion, and he knows it well;
In buying sculpture/ he appraises it '
As he'd appraise a master-mason's work, -
So much for marble, and so much for time,
So much for working tools—but still he buys,
And so he is a patron of the Arts!

CYN. To think that heaven-born Art should be the slave
Of such as he.

PYG.   Well, wealth is heaven-born too,
I work for wealth.

CYN.   Thou workest, love, for fame.

PYG. And fame brings wealth.   The thought's con-
      temptible.   [her.
But I can do more than work for wealth. [*Turns from*

CYN. Such words from one whose noble work it is
To call the senseless marble into life!

PYG. Life!   Dost thou call that life?

CYN.   It all but breathes! (*Sits* L.)

PYG. (*up* R., *bitterly*.)   It all but breathes—therefore it
      talks aloud!
It all but moves—therefore it walks and runs!
It all but lives, and therefore it is life!
No, no, my love, the thing is cold, dull stone,
Shaped to a certain form, but still dull stone,
                    (*Up* R. C., *looking at Statue*.)
The lifeless, senseless mockery of life.
The gods make life, I can make only death!
Why, my Cynisca, though I stand so well,
The merest cut-throat, when he plies his trade,
Makes better death than I with all my skill!

CYN. Hush, my Pygmalion! the gods are good,

And they have made thee nearer unto them
Than other men; this is ingratitude!

PYG. (*haughtily.*) Not so; has not a monarch's second son
More cause for anger that he lacks a throne
Than he whose lot is cast in slavery?   [excuse.

CYN. (*rises.*) Not much more cause, perhaps, but more
Now I must go.

PYG.   So soon, and for so long.

CYN. One day, 'twill quickly pass away!   [doubt,

PYG. With those who measure time by almanacks, no
But not with him who knows no days save those
Born of the sunlight of Cynisca's eyes;
It will be night with me till she returns.

CYN. Then sleep it through, Pygmalion! But stay,
Thou shalt *not* pass the weary hours alone;
Now mark thou this—while I'm away from thee,
There stands my only representative,
(*Indicating* GALATEA, *and withdrawing curtains,*)
She is my proxy, and I charge you, sir,
Be faithful unto her as unto me!
Into her quietly attentive ear
Pour all thy treasures of hyperbole,
And give thy nimble tongue full license, lest
Disuse should rust its glib machinery; [*advancing*
If thoughts of love should haply crowd on thee,
There stands my other self, tell them to her,
She'll listen well; (*he makes a movement of im-*
            Nay, that's ungenerous, [*patience.*)
For she is I, yet lovelier than I,
And hath no temper, sir, and hath no tongue;
Thou hast thy license—make good use of it.
                    (*Crosses* R.)
Already I'm half jealous—there!
        (*draws curtain together concealing statue.*)
                    It's gone.
The thing is but a statue after all,
And I am safe in leaving thee with her;
Farwell, Pygmalion, till I return.
            (*Kisses him, and exit* U. E. R.)

PYG. (*bitterly.*) " The thing is but a statue after all! "
Cynisca little thought that in those words

She touched the key-note of my discontent—
True, I have powers denied other men;
Give me a block of senseless marble—Well,
I'm a magician, and it rests with me
To say what kernal lies within its shell;
It shall contain a man, a woman, a child,
A dozen men and women if I will.
So far the gods and I run neck and neck,
Nay, so far I can beat them at their trade;
I am no bungler—all the men *I* make
Are straight limbed fellows, each magnificent
In the perfection of his manly grace;
I make no crook-backs—all my men are gods,
My women, goddesses, in outward form.
But there's my tether—I can go so far,
And go no farther—at that point I stop,
To curse the bonds that hold me sternly back.
To curse the arrogance of those proud gods,
Who say, " Thou shalt be greatest among men,
" And yet infinitesimally small!"

GALATEA (*from behind curtain* c.) Pygmalion!
PYG. (*after a pause.*) Who called?
GAL.   Pygmalion!

[PYG. *tears away curtain and discovers* GALATEA *alive.*

PYG. Ye gods! It lives!
GAL.   Pygmalion!
PYG.   It speaks!
I have my prayer! my Galatea breathes!
GAL. Where am I? Let me speak, Pygmalion; [warm!
Give me thy hand—both hands—how soft and
Whence came I? (*Descends.*)
PYG.   Why, from yonder pedestal.
GAL. That pedestal! Ah, yes, I recollect.
There was a time when it was part of me.
PYG. That time has passed forever, thou art now
A living, breathing woman, excellent
In every attribute of womankind.
GAL. Where am I, then?
PYG.   Why born into the world
By miracle.

GAL.   Is this the world?
PYG.   It is.
GAL. This room?
PYG.   This room is portion of a house;
The house stands in a grove, the grove itself
Is one of many, many thousand groves
In Athens.
GAL. And is Athens then the world?
PYG. To an Athenian—Yes—
GAL.   And I am one?
PYG. By birth and parentage, not by descent.
GAL. But how came I to be?
PYG.   Well—let me see.
Oh—you were quarried in Pentelicus;
I modelled you in clay—my artisans
Then roughed you out in marble—I, in turn,
Brought my artistic skill to bear on you,
And made you what you are—in all but life—
The gods completed what I had begun,
And gave the only gift I could not give.
GAL. Then is this life?
PYG.   It is.
GAL.   And not long since
I was a cold, dull stone. I recollect
That by some means I knew that I was stone,
That was the first dull gleam of conscience;
I became conscious of a chilly self,
A cold immoveable identity,
I knew that I was stone, and knew no more;
Then, by an imperceptible advance,
Came the dim evidence of outer things,
Seen—darkly and imperfectly—yet seen—
The walls surrounded me, and I, alone,
That pedestal—that curtain—then a voice
That called on Galatea! At that word,
Which seemed to shake my marble to the core,
That which was dim before, came evident.
Sounds, that had hummed around me, indistinct,
Vague, meaningless—seemed to resolve themselves
Into a language I could understand;
I felt my frame pervaded with a glow

That seemed to thaw my marble into flesh;
Its cold hard substance throbbed with active life,
My limbs grew supple, and I moved—I lived;
Lived in the ecstacy of new born life;
Lived in the love of him that fashioned me;
Lived in a thousand tangled thoughts of hope,
Love, gratitude, thoughts that resolved themselves
Into one word, that word, Pygmalion!   (*Kneels to*

PYG.   I have no words to tell thee of my joy,   [*him.*)
O woman—perfect in thy loveliness.

GAL.   What is that word?   Am I a woman?

PYG.   Yes.

GAL.   Art thou a woman?

PYG.   No, I am a man.

GAL.   What *is* a man?

PYG.   A being strongly framed,
To wait on woman, and protect her from
All ills that strength and courage can avert;
To work and toil for her, that she may rest;
To weep and mourn for her, that she may laugh;
To fight and die for her, that she might live!

GAL.   (*after a pause.*)   I'm glad I am a woman.
                    (*Takes his hand—he leads her down* L.)

PYG.   So am I. (*They sit.*)

GAL.   That I escape the pains thou hast to bear?

PYG.   That I may undergo those pains for thee.

GAL.   With whom then would'st thou fight?

PYG.   With any man
Whose word or deed gave Galatea pain.

GAL.   Then there are other men in this strange world?

PYG.   There are indeed.

GAL.   And other women?

PYG.   (*taken aback.*)   Yes;
Though for the moment I'd forgotten it;
Yes, other women.

GAL.   And for all of these
Men work, and toil, and mourn, and weep and fight?

PYG.   It is man's duty, if he's called upon,
To fight for all—he works for those he loves.

GAL.   Then by thy works I know thou lovest me.

PYG.   Indeed, I love thee! (*Embraces her.*)

GAL. With what kind of love?

PYG. I love thee (*recollecting himself and releasing her*)
  as a sculptor does his work!
  (*aside*) There is a diplomacy in that reply.

GAL. My love is different in kind to thine;
  I am no sculptor, and I've done no work,
  Yet I do love thee; say—what love is mine?

PYG. Tell me its symptoms—then I'll answer thee.

GAL. Its symptoms? Let me call them as they come.
  A sense that I am made *by* thee *for* thee,
  That I have no will that is not wholly thine,
  That I've no thought, no hope, no enterprise,
  That does not own thee as its sovereign;
  That I have life, that I may live for thee,
  That I am thine—that thou and I are one!
  What kind of love is that?

PYG.   A kind of love
  That I shall run some risk in dealing with.

GAL. And why, Pygmalion?

PYG.   Such love as thine
  A man may not receive, except indeed
  From one who is, or is to be, his wife.

GAL. Then *I* will be thy wife.

PYG.   That may not be;
  I have a wife—the gods allow but one.

GAL. Why did the gods then send me here to thee?

PYG. I cannot say—unless to punish me (*rises*)
  For unreflecting and presumptuous prayer!
  I prayed that thou should'st live. I have my prayer,
  And now I see the fearful consequence
  That must attend it!

GAL.   Yet thou lovest me? (*Rises.*)

PYG. Who could look on that face and stifle love?

GAL. Then I am beautiful?

PYG.   Indeed thou art.

GAL. I wish that I could look upon myself,
  But that's impossible.

PYG.   Not so indeed, (*crosses* R.)
  This mirror will reflect thy face. Behold!

    (*Hands her a mirror from table* R. C.)

GAL. How beautiful! I am very glad to know
That both our tastes agree so perfectly;
Why, my Pygmalion, I did not think
That aught could be more beautiful than thou,
Till I behold myself (*a pause.*) Believe me, love,
I could look in this mirror all day long.
So I'm a woman.

PYG.   There's no doubt of that!

GAL. Oh happy maid to be so passing fair!
And happier still Pygmalion, who can gaze,
At will, upon so beautiful a face.   [*from her*)

PYG. Hush! Galatea—in thine innocence (*taking glass*
Thou sayest things that others would reprove.

GAL. Indeed, Pygmalion; then it is wrong
To think that one is exquisitely fair?

PYG. Well, Galatea, it's a sentiment
That every woman shares with thee;
They *think* it—but they keep it to themselves.

GAL. And is thy wife as beautiful as I?

PYG. No, Galatea, for in forming thee
I took her features—lovely in themselves—
And in the marble made them lovelier still.

GAL. (*Disappointed.*) Oh! then I'm not original?

PYG.   Well—no—
That is—thou hast indeed a prototype,
But though in stone thou did'st resemble her,
In life, the difference is manifest.

GAL. I'm very glad that I am lovelier than she.
And am I better? (*Sits* L..)

PYG.   That I do not know.

GAL. Then she has faults.

PYG.   Very few indeed;
Mere trivial blemishes, that serve to show
That she and I are of one common kin.
I love her all the better for such faults. [them now.

GAL. (*after a pause.*) Tell me some faults and I'll commit

PYG. There is no hurry; they will come in time; (*sits beside*
Though for that matter, it's a grevious sin [*her* L.)
To sit as lovingly as we sit now.

GAL. *Is* sin so pleasant? If to sit and talk
As we are sitting, be indeed a sin,

Why I could sin all day.   But tell me, love,
Is this great fault that I'm committing now
The kind of fault that only serves to show
That thou and I are of one common kin?

PYG.   Indeed, I'm very much afraid it is.

GAL.   And dost thou love me better for such fault?

PYG.   Where is the mortal that could answer "no?"

GAL.   Why then I'm satisfied, Pygmalion;
Thy wife and I can start on equal terms.
She loves thee?

PYG.   Very much.

GAL.   I'm glad of that.
I like thy wife.

PYG.   And why?

GAL.   (*surprised at the question.*)   Our tastes agree.
We love Pygmalion well, and what is more,
Pygmalion loves us both.   I like thy wife;
I'm sure we shall agree.

PYG.   (*aside.*)   I doubt it much.

GAL.   Is she within?

PYG.   No, she is not within.

GAL.   But she'll come back?

PYG.   Oh, yes, she will come back.

GAL.   How pleased she'll be to know when she returns,
That there was some one here to fill her place. [(*rises*)

PYG.   (*drily.*) Yes, I should say she'd be extremely pleased.

GAL.   Why, there is something in thy voice which says
That thou art jesting.   Is it possible
To say one thing and mean another?

PYG.   Yes,
It's sometimes done.

GAL.   How very wonderful;
So clever!

PYG.   And so very useful.

GAL.   Yes.
Teach me the art.

PYG.   The art will come in time.
My wife will *not* be pleased; there—that's the truth.

GAL.   I do not think that I *shall* like thy wife.
Tell me more of her.

PYG.   Well—

GAL.   What did she say
When last she left thee?

PYG.   Humph! Well, let me see;
Oh! true, she gave thee to me as my wife,—
Her solitary representative;
(*tenderly*) She feared I should be lonely till she came,
And counselled me, if thoughts of love should come,
To speak those thoughts to thee, as I am wont
To speak to her.

GAL.   That's right.

PYG. (*releasing her.*)   But when she spoke
Thou wast a stone, now thou art flesh and blood,
Which makes a difference.

GAL.   It's a strange world;
A woman loves her husband very much,
And cannot brook that I should love him too;
She fears he will be lonely till she comes,
And will not let me cheer his loneliness;
She bids him breathe his love to senseless stone,
And when that stone is brought to life—be dumb!
It's a strange world, I cannot fathom it. (*Crosses* R.)

PYG. (*aside.*)   Let me be brave and put an end to this.
(*aloud.*)   Come Galatea—till my wife returns,
My sister shall provide thee with a home;
Her house is close at hand.

GAL. (*astonished and alarmed.*)   Send me not hence,
Pygmalion—let me stay.

PYG.   It may not be.
Come, Galatea, we shall meet again.

GAL. (*Resignedly.*)   Do with me as thou wilt, Pygmalion!
But we *shall* meet again?—and very soon?

PYG. Yes, very soon.

GAL.   And when thy wife returns,
She'll let me stay with thee?

PYG.   I do not know. [alas!
(*aside*) Why should I hide the truth from her (*aloud*)
I may *not* see thee then.

GAL.   Pygmalion!
What fearful words are these?

PYG.   The bitter truth.
I may not love thee—I must send thee hence.

GAL.　Recall those words, Pygmalion, my love!
　　　　Was it for this that heaven gave me life?
　　　　Pygmalion, have mercy on me; see
　　　　I am thy work, thou hast created me;
　　　　The gods have sent me to thee.　I am thine,
　　　　Thine! only, and unalterably thine! (*music*)
　　　　This is the thought with which my soul is charged.
　　　　Thou tellest me of one who claims thy love,
　　　　That thou hast love for her alone.　Alas!
　　　　I do not know these things—I only know
　　　　That heaven has sent me here to be with thee,
　　　　Thou tellest me of duty to thy wife,
　　　　Of vows that thou will love but her; Alas!
　　　　I do not know these things—I only know
　　　　That heaven, who sent me here, has given me
　　　　One all absorbing duty to discharge—
　　　　To love thee, and to make thee love again.

[*During this speech* PYGMALION *has shown symptoms of
　irresolution; at its conclusion he takes her in his arms,
　and embraces her passionately.*]

ACT DROP.

[*Ring when* PYGMALION *kisses* GALATEA.]

ACT II.

SCENE: SAME AS ACT I.

[*See that curtains that concealed the statue are closed.*]
[PYGMALION *discovered at work on an unfinished statue* L.]

PYG.　To-morrow my Cynisca comes to me;
　　　　Would that she had never departed hence!
　　　　It took a miracle to make me false,
　　　　And even then I was but false in thought;
　　　　A less exacting wife might be appeased
　　　　By that reflection.　But Pygmalion

Must be immaculate in every thought,
Even though Heaven's armaments be ranged
Against the fortress of his constancy.

Enter MYRINE, L. E. R., *in great excitement.*

MYR. Pygmalion!
PYG.   Myrine!
MYR. (*shrinking from him.*)   Touch me not,
Thou hast deceived me, and deceived thy wife!
Who is the woman thou didst send to me
To share my roof last night?
PYG.   Be pacified;
Judge neither of us hastily, in truth
She is as pure, as innocent as thou.
MYR. Oh, miserable man—confess the truth,
Disguise not that of which she boasts aloud.
PYG. Of what then does she boast?
MYR.   To all I say
She answers with one parrot-like reply,
" I love Pygmalion "—and when incensed
I tell her that thou hast a cheated wife,
She only says " I love Pygmalion,
" I and my life are. his, and his alone!"
Who is this shameless woman, sir?   Confess!
PYG. Myrine, I will tell thee all.   The gods
To punish my expressed impiety,
Have worked a miracle, and brought to life
My statue Galatea.
MYR. (*incredulously.*)   Marvellous,
If it be true!
PYG.   It's absolutely true.
(MYRINE *opens the curtains and sees the pedestal empty.*)
MYR. The statue's gone! (GALATEA *appears at door* R. U. E.]
PYG.   The statue's at the door!
GAL. (*coming down and embracing him*)—
At last we meet!   Oh! my Pygmalion!
What strange, strange things have happened since
       we met.
PYG. Why, what has happened to thee?
GAL.   Fearful things!
(*to* MYR.) I went with thee into thine house—

MYR.   Well, well.

GAL. And then I sat alone and wept—and wept
A long, long time for my Pygmalion.
Then by degrees—by tedious degrees,
The light—the glorious light!—the godsent light!
I saw it sink—sink—sink—behind the world;
Then I grew cold—cold—as I used to be,
Before my loved Pygmalion gave me life.   •
Then came the fearful thought that, by degrees,
I was returning into stone again!
How bitterly I wept and prayed aloud
That it might not be so!   "Spare me, ye gods!
"Spare me," I cried, "for my Pygmalion,
"A little longer for Pygmalion!
"Oh, take me not so early from my love;
"Oh, let me see him once—but once again!"
But no—they heard me not, for they are good,
And had they heard, must needs have pitied me;
They had not seen *thee* and they did not know
The happiness that I must leave behind.
I fell upon thy couch (*to* MYRINE), my eyelids closed,
My senses faded from me one by one;
I knew no more until I found myself,
After a strange dark interval of time,
Once more upon my hated pedestal,
A statue—motionless—insensible;
And then I saw the glorious gods come down!
Down to this room! the air was filled with them!
They came and looked upon Pygmalion,
And looking on him, kissed him one by one,
And said, in tones that spoke to me of life,
"We cannot take her from such happiness!
"Live Galatea for his love!"   And then
The glorious light that I had lost came back—
There was Myrine's room, there was her couch,
There was the sun in heaven; and the birds
Sang once more in the great green waving trees,
As I had heard them sing—I lived once more
To look on him I love!

MYR.   'Twas but a dream! (*coming down* R.)
Once every day this death occurs to us,

Till thou and I and all who dwell on earth,
Shall sleep to wake no more!

GAL. (*horrified, takes* MYRINE's *hand.*) To wake no more!

PYG. That time must come, may be not yet awhile,
Still it must come, and we shall all return
To the cold earth from which we quarried thee,

GAL. See how the promises of new-born life
  • Fade from the bright hope-picture, one by one!
Love for Pygmalion—a blighting sin,
His love a shame that he must hide away.
Sleep, stone-like senseless sleep, our natural state,
And life a passing vision born thereof,
From which we wake to native senselessness!
How the bright promises fade one by one!

MYR. Why there are many men who thou mayest love;
But not Pygmalion—he has a wife.

GAL. Does no one love him?

MYR.   Certainly—*I* do.
He is my brother.

GAL.   Did he give thee life?

MYR. Why, no, but then—

GAL.   He did not give thee life,
And yet thou lovest him!   And why not I ?
Who owe my very being to his love.

PYG. Well, thou mayest love me—as a father.

MYR.   Yes;
He is thy father, for he gave thee life.

GAL. Well, as thou wilt, it is enough to know
That I may love thee.   Wilt thou love me too?

PYG. Yes, as a daughter; there, that's understood.

GAL. Then I am satisfied (*kissing his hand.*)

MYR. (*aside.*)   Indeed I hope
Cynisca also will be satisfied!

                    Exit R. I. E. PYG. *crosses* R.

GAL. (*To* PYG., *who crosses* R.) Thou art not going from me?

PYG.   For awhile.

GAL. Oh, take me with thee; leave me not alone
With these cold emblems of my former self.

                    (*alluding to statues.*)

I dare not look on them!

PYG.   Leucippe comes,

And he shall comfort thee till I return;
I'll not be long!

GAL.   Leucippe! Who is he?

PYG. A valiant soldier.

GAL.   What is that?

PYG.   A man,
Who's hired to kill his country's enemies.

GAL. (*horrified.*) A paid assassin!

PYG. (*amazed.*) Well, that's rather strong.
There spoke the thoroughly untutored mind;
So coarse a sentiment might fairly pass
With mere Arcadians—a cultured state
Holds soldiers at a higher estimate.
In Athens—which is highly civilized—
The soldier's social rank is in itself
Almost a patent of nobility.

GAL. He kills! And he is paid to kill!

PYG.   No doubt.
But then he kills to save his countrymen.

GAL. Whether his countrymen be right or wrong?

PYG. He don't go into that—it's quite enough
That there are enemies for him to kill;
He goes and kills them when his orders come.

GAL. How terrible! Why, my Pygmalion,
How many dreadful things thou teachest me;
Thou tellest me of death—that hideous doom
That all must fill; and having told me this—
Here is a man, whose business is to kill;
To filch from other men the priceless boon
That thou hast given me—the boon of life.
And thou defendest him.

PYG.   I have no time
To make these matters clear—but here he comes,
Talk to him—thou wilt find him kind and good,
Despite his terrible profession.

GAL. (*in great terror.*)   No!
I'll not be left with him, Pygmalion. Stay!
He is a murderer!

PYG.   Ridiculous!
Why, Galatea, he will harm thee not,

He is as good as brave. I'll not be long,
I'll soon return.   Farewell!   [*Exit* U. E. R.
GAL.   I will obey
Since thou desirest it; but to be left
Alone with one whose mission is to kill!
Oh, it is terrible!

Enter LEUCIPPE R. U. E., *with a Fawn* that he has shot.*

LEUC.   A splendid shot,
And one that I shall never make again!   [*ner.*
GAL. Monster! Approach me not! (*Shrinking into* L. *cor-*
LEUC.   Why, who is this?
Nay, I'll not hurt thee, maiden!
GAL.   Spare me, sir!
I have not done thy country any wrong,
I am no enemy!
LEUC.   I'll swear to that!
Were Athens' enemies as fair as thou,
She'd never be at loss for warriors.
GAL. Oh miserable man, repent! repent!
Ere the stern marble claim you once again.
LEUC. I don't quite understand—
GAL.   Remember, sir,
The sculptor who designed you, little thought
That when he prayed the gods to give you life,
He turned a monster loose upon the world.
See, there is blood upon those cruel hands!
Oh touch me not.
LEUC. (*aside.*)   Poor crazy little girl!   [not—
Why—there's no cause for fear—I'll harm thee
As for the blood, this will account for it (*showing*
GAL. What's that?   [*Fawn.*)
LEUC.   A little Fawn.
GAL.   It does not move!
LEUC. No, for I wounded her.
GAL.   Oh, horrible!

---

* NOTE.—This Fawn must be perfectly limp and death-like, and
at the same time a pretty and interesting object, or the scene
which follows will excite ridicule. The Fawn used at the Hay-
market Theatre was supplied by Mr. H. Ward, Naturalist, 2,
Vere Street, Oxford Street.

LEUC. Poor little thing!   'Twas almost accident;
    I lay upon my back beneath a tree,
    Whistling the lazy hours away—when lo!
    I saw her bounding through a distant glade;
    My bow was handy; in sheer wantonness
    I aimed an arrow at her, and let fly,
    Believing that at near a hundred yards
    So small a being would be safe enough,
    But, strange to tell, I hit her.   Here she is;
    She moves—poor little lady!   Ah, she's dead!
GAL. Oh, horrible! oh, miserable man!   [*arms*)—
    What have you done—(*Takes Fawn into her*
                Why you have murdered her!
    Poor little thing!   I know not what thou art;
    Thy form is strange to me; but thou hadst life
    And he has robbed thee of it!
    (*Strokes Fawn with her handkerchief and gives it*
                            [*back to* LEUC.)
        (*Suddenly.*)   Get you hence!
    Ere vengeance overtake you!
LEUC.   Well, in truth,
    I have some apprehension on that score.
    It was Myrine's—though I knew it not.
    'Twould pain her much to know that it is dead;
    So keep the matter carefully from her   [*hind.*]
    Until I can replace it. [*Exit* LEUCIPPE, R. U. E., *with*
GAL.   Get you hence;
    I have no compact with a murderer!

Enter MYRINE, R. I. E.

MYR. Why, Galatea, what has frightened thee?
GAL. Myrine, I have that to say to thee
    That thou must nerve thyself to hear.   That man—
    That man thou lovest—is a murderer!
MYR. Poor little maid!   Pygmalion, ere he left,
    Told me that by that name thou didst describe
    The bravest soldier that our country owns!
    He's no assassin, he's a warrior.
GAL. Then what is an assassin?
MYR.   One who wars
    Only with weak, defenceless creatures.   One

Whose calling is to murder unawares.
My brave Leucippe is no murderer.

GAL. Thy brave Leucippe is no longer brave,
He is a mere assassin by thy showing.
I saw him with his victim in his arms,
His wicked hands dyed crimson with her blood;
There she lay, cold and stark, her gentle eyes
Glazed with the film of death.   She moved but once,
She turned her head to him and tried to speak,
But ere she could articulate a word,
Her head fell helplessly, and she was dead!

MYR. Why, you are raving, girl.   Who told you this?

GAL. He owned it; and he gloried in the deed.
He told me how, in arrant wantonness,
He drew his bow, and smote her to the heart.

MYR. *Leucippe* did all this!   Impossible!
You must be dreaming!

GAL.   On my life it's true.
See here's a handkerchief which still stained
With her blood—I staunched it with my hand.

MYR. Who was his victim?

GAL.   Nay—I cannot tell.
Her form was strange to me—but here he comes;
Oh! hide me from that wicked murderer! (*Crosses* L.)

Enter LEUCIPPE, U. E. R.

MYR. Leucippe can this dreadful tale be true?

LEUC. (*to* GAL. *aside.*) Thou should have kept my secret.
See, poor girl,
How it distresses her.   (*To* MYR.) It's true enough,
But Galatea should have kept it close,
I knew that it would pain thee greviously;

MYR. Some devil must have turned Leucippe's brain;
You did all this?

LEUC.   Undoubtedly I did.
I saw my victim dancing happily
Across my field of view—I took my bow,
And, at the distance of a hundred yards,
I sent an arrow right into her heart.
There are few soldiers who could do as much.

MYR. Indeed I hope that there are very few.
Oh, miserable man!

LEUC.   That's rather hard.
Congratulate me rather on my aim,
Of which I have some reason now to boast;
As for my victim—why, one more or less,
What does it matter? There are plenty left!
And then reflect. Indeed, I never thought
That I should hit her at so long a range;
My aim was truer than I thought it was,
And the poor little lady's dead!

MYR.   Alas!
This is the calmness of insanity.
What shall we do? Go, hide yourself away.

LEUC. But——

MYR.   Not a word, I will not hear thy voice,
I will not look upon thy face again;
Begone! (*sits at table*, R., *and sobs.*)

GAL.   Go, sir, or I'll alarm the house!

LEUC. Well, this is sensibility, indeed!
Well, they are women—women judge these things
By some disjointed logic of their own.
I'm off to Athens—when your reason comes
Send for me, if you will. Till then, farewell.

                    [*Exit* U. E. R., *angrily.*

MYR. Oh, this must be a dream, and I shall wake
To happiness once more!

GAL. (*jumping at the idea.*) A dream! no doubt!
We both are dreaming, and we dream the same,
But by what sign, Myrine, can we tell
Whether we dream or wake?

MYR.   There are some things
Too terrible for truth, and this is one.

Enter PYGMALION, R. E. U., *with the hind.*

PYG. (*down* C.)—Why, what's the matter with Leucippe,
    girl?
I saw him leave the house, and mount his horse
With every show of anger.

MYR. A fearful thing has happened. He is ma

And hath done a deed I dare not name.
Did he say ought to thee before he left?

PYG. Yes; when I asked him what had angered him,
He threw me this (*showing hind.*)

GAL. (*in extreme horror*)—His victim—take it hence.
I cannot look at it.

MYR.   Why what is this?

GAL. The being he destroyed in very wantonness;
He robbed it of the life the gods had given.
Oh! take it hence, I dare not look on death!

(PYGMALION *throws him on chair* R.)

MYR. Why was this *all* he killed?

GAL. (*astonished.*)   All ! ! ! And enough!

MRY. Why, girl—thou must be mad! Pygmalion—
She told me he had murdered somebody,
But knew not whom!

PYG. (*in great agitation.*)   The girl will drive us mad!
Bid them prepare my horse—I'll bring him back.

[*Exit* MYRINE, L. E. R., *running.*

GAL. Have I done wrong? Indeed I did not know;
Thou art not angry with me?

PYG.   Yes, I am;
I'm more than angry with thee—not content
With publishing thine unmasked love for me,
Thou hast estranged Leucippe from *his* love
Through thine unwarrantable foolishness.

Enter MIMOS, U. E. R.

MIM. Sir, Chrysos and his lady are without.

PYG. I cannot see them now. Stay—show them in.

[*Exit* MIMOS.

(*To* GAL.) Go wait in there. I'll join thee very soon.

[*Exit* GALATEA, L. E. R.

Enter DAPHNE U. E. R.

(PYGMALION *goes to statue*, L, *and begins to work on it.*)

DAPH. Where is Pygmalion?

PYG.   Pygmalion's here.

DAPH. We called upon you many months ago,

But you were not at home—so being here,
We looked around us and we saw the stone,
You keep so carefully behind that veil.

PYG. That was a most outrageous liberty.

DAPH. Sir! do you know me?

PYG.   You are Chrysos' wife.
Has Chrysos come with you?

DAPH.   He waits without.
I am his herald to prepare you for
The honor he confers. Be civil, sir,
And he may buy that statue; if he does
Your fortune's made!

PYG. (*To* MIMOS.) You'd better send him in. [*Exit* MIM., R.

Enter CHRYSOS, U. E. R.

CHRY. (*Down* R. C.) Well—is the young man's mind prepared?

DAPH.   It is;
He seems quite calm. Give money for the stone,
I've heard that it is far beyond all price,
But run it down, abuse it ere you buy.

CHRY. (*to* PYG.) Where is the statue that I saw last time?

PYG. (*at a loss*.) Sir, it's unfinished—its a clumsy thing.
I am ashamed of it.

CHRY.   It isn't good.
There's want of tone; it's much too hard and thin;
Then the half distances are very crude—
Oh—very crude indeed—then it lacks air,
And wind and motion, massive light and shade;
It's very roughly scumbled; on my soul
The scumbling's damnable!

DAPH. (*aside to him*.)   Bethink yourself!
That's said of painting—this is sculpture!

CHRY.   Eh?
It's the same thing, the principle's the same.
Now for its price. Let's see—what will it weigh?

DAPH. A ton, or thereabouts.

CHRY.   Suppose we say
A thousand drachmas?

PYG.   No, no, no, my lord;

The work is very crude and thin, and then,
Remember, sir, the scumbling—

CHRY.   Damnable!
But never mind, although the thing is poor,
'Twill serve to hold a candle in my hall.

PYG. Excuse me, sir; poor though that statue be,
I value it beyond all price.

CHRY.   Pooh, pooh!
I give a thousand drachmas for a stone
Which in the rough would not fetch half that sum!

DAPH. Why bless my soul, young man, are you aware
We gave but fifteen hundred not long since
For an Apollo twice as big as that!

PYG. But pardon me, a sculptor does not test
The beauty of a figure by its bulk.

CHRY. Ah! then *she* does.

DAPH.   Young man, you'd best take care,
You are offending Chrysos!   [*Exit* R. C. L.

CHRY.   And his wife. (*going*)

PYG. I cannot stay to enter into that   [*door* L.
Sir, once for all, the statue's not for sale. [*Exit* 2

CHRY. Sir, once for all, I will not be denied;
Confound it—if a patron of the arts
Is thus to be dictated to *by* art,
What comes of that art patron's patronage?
Oh, upstart vanity of human kind!
Oh, pride of worms—oh, scholarship of fools!
Oh, ponderosity of atoms! oh,
Substantiality of nothingness!
He must be taught a lesson—Where's the stone!

                    (*Goes to pedestal and opens curtains.*)

It's gone. (*Enter* GALATEA, R. I. E., *he stares at
her in astonishment.*) Hallo! What's this?

GAL.   Are you unwell?

CHRY. Oh, no—I fancied just at first—pooh, pooh!
Ridiculous. (*aside*) And yet it's very like!
(*aloud.*) I know your face, have'nt I seen you in
In—in (*puzzling himself.*)

GAL.   In marble? Very probably.   [this must be

CHRY. (*recovering himself.*) Oh, now I understand. Why

Pygmalion's model!   Yes, of course it is.
A very bold faced woman, I'll be bound.
These models always are.   Her face, alas,
Is very fair; her figure, too, is neat;
But, notwithstanding, I will speak with her.
Come hither, maiden.

GAL. (*Who has been examining him in great wonder.*)
    Tell me, what *are* you?

CHRY. What *am* I?

GAL.   Yes, I mean, are you a man?

CHRY. Well, yes; I'm told so.

GAL.   Then believe them not,
They've been deceiving you.

CHRY.   The deuce they have!

GAL. A man is very tall, and straight, and strong,
With big brave eyes, fair face, and tender voice.
I've see one.

CHRY.   *Have* you?

GAL.   Yes, you are no man.

CHRY. Does the young person take me for a woman?

GAL. A woman?   No; a woman's soft and weak,
And fair, and exquisitely beautiful.
I am a woman, you are not like me.

CHRY. The gods forbid that I should be like you,
And farm my features at so much an hour!

GAL. And yet I like you, for you make me laugh;
You are so round and red, your eyes so small,
Your mouth so large, your face so seared with lines,
And then you are so little and so fat!

CHRY. (*aside.*)   This is a most extraordinary girl.

GAL. Oh, stay—I understand—Pygmalion's skill
Is the result of long experience.
The individual who modelled you
Was a beginner very probably?

CHRY. (*puzzled.*) No. I have seven elder brothers. Strange
That one so young should be so very bold. (*Crosses* L.)

GAL. (*Surprised*)—This is not boldness, it is innocence;
Pygmalion says so, and he ought to know.

CHRY. No doubt, but I was not born yesterday.   (*Sits* L.)

GAL. Indeed!—*I was*. (*He beckons her to sit beside him.*)
    How awkwardly you sit.

CHRY. I'm not aware that there is anything
    Extraordinary in my sitting down.
    The nature of the seated attitude
    Does not leave scope for much variety.
GAL. I never saw Pygmalion sit like that.
CHRY. Don't he sit down like other men?
GAL.   Of course!
    He always puts his arm around my waist.
CHRY. The deuce he does! Artistic reprobate!
GAL. But you do not. Perhaps you don't know how?
CHRY. Oh yes; I *do* know how!
GAL.   Well, do it then!
CHRY. It's a strange whim, but I will humor her (*does so.*)
    You're sure it's innocence?
GAL.   Of course it is.
    I tell you I was born but yesterday.
CHRY. Who is your mother?
GAL.   Mother! what is that?
    I never had one. I'm Pygmalion's child;
    Have people usually mothers?
CHRY.   Well
    That is the rule.
GAL.   But then Pygmalion
    Is cleverer than most men.
CHRY.   Yes I've heard
    That he has powers denied to other men,
    And I'm beginning to believe it! (*Aside.*)

Enter DAPHNE, U. E. R.

DAPH.   Why   [GAL.
    What's this? (CHRYSOS *quickly moves away from*
CHRY.   My wife?
DAPH.   Can I believe my eyes? (GAL. *rises.*)
CHRY. No!
DAPH. Who's this woman? Why, how very like——
CHRY. Like what?
DAPH.   That statue that we wished to buy,
    The self-same face, the self-same drapery,
    In every detail it's identical.
    Why, one would almost think Pygmalion,

By some strange means, had brought the thing to
So marvellous her likeness to that stone.   [life,

CHRY. (*aside.*) A very good idea, and one that I
May well improve upon. It's rather rash,
But desperate ills need desperate remedies. [*to her.*)
Now for a good one. Daphne, calm yourself, (*crosses*
You know the statue that we spoke of. Well,
The gods have worked a miracle on it
And it has come to life. Behold it here!

DAPH. Bah! Do you think me mad?

GAL.   His tale is true.
I was a cold unfeeling block of stone,
Inanimate—insensible—until
Pygmalion, by the ardour of his prayers
Kindled the spark of life within my frame
And made me what I am!

CHRY. (*aside to* GAL.)   That's very good;
Go on and keep it up.

DAPH.   You brazen girl,
I am his wife!

GAL.   His wife? (*To* CHRYsos.) Then get you hence.
I may not love you when your wife is here.

DAPH. Why, what unknown audacity is this?

CHRY. It's the audacity of innocence;
Don't judge her by the rules that govern you,
She was born yesterday, and you were *not!*

Enter MIMOS, U. E. R.

MIM. My lord, Pygmalion's here.

CHRY. (*aside.*)   He'll ruin all.

DAPH. (*to* MIMOS.) Who is this woman?

CHRY.   Why, I've told you, she——

DAPH. Stop, not a word! I'll have it from *his* lips!

GAL. Why ask him when I tell you?

DAPH.   Hold your tongue!
(*To* MIMOS.) Who is this woman? If you tell a lie
I'll have you whipped.

MIM.   Oh, I shall tell no lie!
That is a statue that has come to life.

CHRY. (*crosses and aside to* MIMOS) I'm very much obliged
to you. (*Gives him money.*)

Enter MYRINE, U. E. R.

MYR.   What's this?
Is anything the matter?
DAPH.   Certainly.
This woman——
MYR.   Is a statue come to life.
CHRY. I'm very much obliged to *you!* (*Crosses to her.*)

Enter PYGMALION, U. E. R.

PYG.   How now
Chrysos? (*Down* C.)
CHRY.   The statue!——
DAPH.   Stop!
CHRY.   Let me explain.
The statue that I purchased——
DAPH.   Let me speak.
Chrysos—this girl, Myrine, and your slave,
Have all agreed to tell me that she is——
PYG. The statue, Galatea, come to life?
Undoubtedly she is!
CHRY.   It seems to me,   [DAPHNE.)
I'm very much obliged to every one! (*Crosses to*

Enter CYNISCA, U. E. R.

CYN. Pygmalion, my love!
PYG.   Cynisca here!
CYN. And even earlier than hoped to be.   [pardon, sir.
(*Aside.*) Why who are these? (*aloud.*) I beg your
I thought my husband was alone.
DAPH.(*Maliciously.*)   No doubt.
I also thought *my* husband was alone;
We wives are too confiding.
CYN. (*Aside to* PYGMALION)—Who are these?
PYG. Why, this is Chrysos, this is Daphne. They
Have come—
DAPH.   On very different errands, sir. [girl;
(*To* GALATEA) Chrysos has come to see this brazen
I have come after Chrysos—
CHRY.   As you keep
So strictly to the sequence of events
Add this—Pygmalion came after *you!*

Cyn. Who is this lady (*alluding to* Galatea?) Why,
 impossible!
Daph. Oh, not at all! (*goes up* r. *with* Chrysos.)
Cyn. (*Turning to pedestal*)—And yet the statue's gone!
Pyg. Cynisca, miracles have taken place;
 The gods have given Galatea life!
Cyn. Oh, marvellous! Is this indeed the form
 That my Pygmalion fashioned with his hands?
 (*Approaching* Galatea *with great admiration.*)
Pyg. Indeed it is.
Cyn.   Why, let me look (*Crosses to* Galatea.)
 Yes, it's the same fair face—the same fair form;
 Clad in the same fair folds of drapery!
Gal. And dost thou know me then?
Cyn.   Hear her! she speaks!
 Our Galatea speaks aloud! know thee?
 Why, I have sat for hours, and watched thee grow,
 Sat—motionless as thou—wrapped in his work,
 Save only that in very ecstacy
 I hurried ever and anon to kiss
 The glorious hands that made thee all thou art! [*her.*)
 Come—let me kiss thee with a sister's love (*kisses*
 See, she can kiss.
Daph. (r.)   Yes, I'll be bound she can!
Cyn. Why my Pygmalion, where's the joy
 That ought to animate the face of thine,
 Now that the gods have crowned thy wondrous skill.
Chry. (*who has crossed behind to* Pygmalion.) Stick to our
         story; bold faced though she be [*alluding to* Gal-
 She's very young, and may perhaps repent;   [atea,
 It's terrible to have to tell a lie,
 But if it must be told—why, tell it well!
                    (*Goes up* r. *and sits.*)
Cyn. (*getting angry.*) I see it all. I have returned too soon.
Daph. (r.)   No, I'm afraid you have returned too late;
 Cynisca, never leave that man again,
 Or leave him altogether!
Cyn. (*astonished.*)   Why, what's this?
Daph. Our husbands don't deserve such wives as we,
 I'll set you an example! (*going.*)
Chry. (*calmly.*)   Well, my dear,

I've no objection to your leaving me;
I've brought it on myself.

DAPH.   Then I'll go home,
And bolt the doors, and leave you——

CHRY. (*alarmed.*)   Where!

DAPH.   Outside! (*Exit* U. E. R.)
          (CHRYSOS, *after a pause, follows her.*)

CYN. (*To* PYG.) Hast thou been false to all I said to thee
Before I left?

GAL. (R.)   Oh, madam, bear with him,
Judge him not hastily; in every word,
In every thought he has obeyed thy wish.
Thou badst him to speak to me as unto thee;
And he and I have sat as lovingly
As if thou had'st been present to behold   [PYG.
How faithfully thy wishes were obeyed! [*Crosses to*

CYN. (R.) Pygmalion! What is this?

PYG. (L., *to* GAL.)   Go, get thee hence,
Thou shouldst not see the fearful consequence
That must attend those heedless words of thine!

GAL. (C.) Judge him not hastily, he's not like this
When he and I are sitting here alone.
He has two voices and two faces, Madam,
One for the world, and one for him and me!

CYN. (*with suppressed passion, crosses to* PYG.) Thy wife
          against thine eyes!   Those are the stakes!
Well, thou hast played thy game, and thou has lost,

PYG. Cynisca, hear me!   In a cursed hour
I prayed for power to give that statue life.
My impious prayer aroused the outraged gods,—
They are my judges, leave me in their hands.
I have been false to them, but not to thee!
Spare me!

CYN.   Oh, pitiful adventurer!
He dares to lose but does not dare to pay.
Come, be a man!   See, *I* am brave enough
And I have more to bear than thou!   Behold!
I am alone, thou hast thy statue bride!
Oh, Artemis, my mistress, hear me now
Ere I remember how I love that man,
And in that memory forget my shame.

If he in deed or thought hath been untrue,
Be just and let him pay the penalty!

(PYGMALION *with an exclamation covers his eyes with his hands.*)

GAL. Cynisca, pity him!　(*Crosses to her and kneels.*)
CYN. I know no pity, woman; for the act
That thawed thee into flesh has hardened me
Into the cursed stone from which thou cam'st.
We have changed places; from this moment forth
Be thou the wife and I the senseless stone!

(*Thrusts* GALATEA *from her.*)

END OF ACT II.　　[QUICK DROP.]

ACT III.

SCENE: SAME AS ACTS I. AND II.

[See Curtains to Pedestal open.]

Enter DAPHNE, U. E. R.

DAPH. It seems Pygmalion *has* the fearful gift
Of bringing stone to life.　I'll question him
And ascertain how far that power extends.

Enter MYRINE, I. E. L., *weeping.*

Myrine—and in tears!　Why, what's amiss?
MYR. Oh, we were all so happy yesterday,
And now, within twelve miserable hours,
A blight has fallen upon all of us.
Pygmalion is blind as death itself—
Cynisca leaves his home this very day—
And my Leucippe hath deserted me!
I shall go mad with all this weight of grief!
DAPH. All this is Galatea's work?
MYR.　　　　　　　　　Yes, all.

DAPH. But can't you stop her? Shut the creature up,
  Dispose of her, or break her? Won't she chip?
MYR. No, I'm afraid not.
DAPH.   Ah, were I his wife,
  I'd spoil her beauty! There'd be little chance
  Of finding him and her alone again!
MYR. There's little need to take precautions now,
  For he, alas, is blind.
DAPH.   Blind! What of that?
  Man has five senses; if he loses one
  The vital energy on which it fed
  Goes to intensify the other four.
  He had five arrows in his quiver; well,
  He has shot one away, and four remain.
  My dear, an enemy is not disarmed
  Because he's lost one arrow out of five.
MYR. The punishment he undergoes might well
  Content his wife!
DAPH.   A happy woman that!
MYR. Cynisca happy?
DAPH.   To be sure she is;
  She has the power to punish faithlessness,
  And she has used it on her faithless spouse.
  Had I Cynisca's privilege, I swear
  I'd never let my Chrysos rest in peace,
  Until he warranted my using it!
  Pygmalion's wronged her, and she's punished him,
  What more could woman want?

Enter CYNISCA, *2nd door* L.

CYN. (*coming forward.*) What more? Why this!
  The power to tame my tongue to speak the words
  That would restore him to his former self!
  The power to quell the fierce, unruly soul
  That battles with my miserable heart!
  The power to say, "Oh, my Pygmalion,
  " My love is thine to hold or cast away,
  " Do with it as thou wilt; it cannot die!"
  I'd barter half my miserable life
  For power to say these few true words to him!

MYR. Why, then there's hope for him!
CYN.   There's none indeed!
This day I'll leave his home and hide away
Where I can brood upon my shame.   I'll fan
The smouldering fire of jealousy until
It bursts forth into an all-devouring flame,
And pray that I may perish in its glow! (*Crosses* L.)
DAPH. That's bravely said, Cynisca!   Never fear;
Pygmalion will give thee wherewithal
To nurture it.
CYN. (*passionately*, *crosses to* C.) I need not wherewithal!
I carry wherewithal within my heart!
Oh, I can conjure up the scene at will
When he and she sit lovingly alone.
I know too well the devilish art he works,
And how his guilty passion shapes itself.
I follow him through every twist and turn,
By which he wormed himself into *my* heart;
I hear him breathing to the guilty girl
The fond familiar nothings of *our* love;
I hear him whispering into *her* ear
The tenderness that he rehearsed on me.
I follow him through all his well-known moods—
Now fierce and passionate, now fanciful,
And ever tuning his accursed tongue
To chime in with the passion at her heart.
Oh, never fear that I shall starve the flame!
When jealousy takes shelter in *my* heart,
It does not die for lack of sustenance! (*Crosses* R.)
DAPH. Come to my home, and thou shall feed it there;
We'll play at widows, and we'll pass our time
Railing against the perfidy of man.
CYN. But Chrysos?——
DAPH.   Chrysos?   Oh, you won't see him?
CYN. How so?
DAPH.   How so?   I've turned him out of doors!
Why, does the girl consider jealousy
Her unassailable prerogative?
Thou hast thy vengeance on Pygmalion—
He can no longer feast upon *thy* face.
Well, Chrysos can no longer feast on mine!

I can't *put out* his eyes, I wish I could;
But I can *shut* them out, and that I've done.

CYN. I thank you madam, and I'll go with you (*Goes up.*)

MYR. No, no; thou shalt not leave Pygmalion; (*Crosses to*
He will not live if thou desertest him.　　　[CYN.
Add nothing to his pain—this second blow
Might well complete the work thou hast begun!

CYN. Nay, let me go—I must not see his face;
For if I look on him I may relent.
Detain me not, Myrine—fare thee well!

> [*Exit* U. E. R., MYRINE *follows her.*]

DAPH. Well, there'll be pretty scenes in Athens now
That statues may be vivified at will.

> (CHRYSOS *enters* U. E. R., *unobserved.*)

Why, I have daughters—all of them of age—
What chance is there for plain young women, now
That every man may take a block of stone
And carve a family to suit his tastes?

CHRY. If every woman were a Daphne, man
Would never care to look on sculptured stone.
(*Sentimentally.*)　　Oh, Daphne!

DAPH.　　　　　　　　　Monster—get you hence, away!
I'll hold no converse with you, get you gone.
(*Aside.*) If I'd Cynisca's tongue I'd wither him!
(*Imitating* CYNISCA.) "Oh, I can conjure up the scene
"Where you and she sit lovingly alone!　　[at will
"Oh, never fear that I will starve the flame;
"When jealousy takes shelter in *my* heart,
"It does not die for lack of sustenance!"

CHRY. I'm sure of that! your hospitality
Is well renowned.　Extend it, love, to me!
Oh, take me home again!

DAPH.　　　　　　　　　Home! no, not I!
Why, I've a gallery of goddesses,
Fifty at least—half dressed bacchantes, too—
Dryads and water nymphs of every kind;
Suppose I find when I go home to-day,
That they've all taken it into *their* heads
To come to life—what would become of them,
Or me, with Chrysos in the house?　No—no,

They're bad enough in marble—but in flesh !!!
I'll sell the bold-faced hussies one and all,
But till I've sold them, Chrysos stops outside!

CHRY. What *have* I done?

DAPH. What have you done, sir.

CHRY. I cannot tell you—it would take too long!

DAPH. I saw you sitting with that marble minx,
Your arm pressed lovingly around her waist.
Explain *that* Chrysos.

CHRY. It explains itself;
I am a patron of the arts, my dear,
And I am very fond of statuary.

DAPH. Bah—I've artistic tastes as well as you,
But still, you never saw *me* sitting with
My arms around a stone Apollo's waist!
As for this " statue "—could I see her now,
I'd test your taste for fragments!

CHRY. Spare the girl,
She's very young and very innocent,
She claims your pity.

DAPH. Does she?

CHRY. Yes, she does.
If I saw Daphne sitting with her arm
Round an Apollo, I should pity *him*.
(*Putting his arm around her waist.*)

DAPH. (*relenting.*) *Would* you?

CHRY. I should, upon my word, I should.

DAPH. Well, Chrysos, thou art pardoned. (*Embraces him.*)
The circumstances were exceptional. [After all

CHRY. (*aside.*) Unhappily, they were!

DAPH. Come home, but mind,
I'll sell my gallery of goddesses;
No good can come of animating stone. (*Goes up* R.C.)

CHRY. Oh pardon me—why every soul on earth
· Sprang from the stones Deucalion threw behind.
(*Goes up and looks at statue* R.)

DAPH. But then Deucalion only threw the stones,
He left it to the gods to fashion them.

CHRY. (*aside—looking at her.*) And we who've seen the
work the gods turned out,

Would rather leave it to Pygmalion!   [*Venus.*)

DAPH. (*taking* CHRYSOS' *arm, who is looking at a statue of*
Come along, do!   [*Exeunt,* U. E. R.

Enter MYRINE, I. E. L., *in great distress.*

MYR. Pygmalion's heard that he must lose his wife,
And swears, by all the gods that reign above,
He will not live if she deserts him now!
What—what is to be done?

Enter GALATEA, I. E. R.

GAL.   Myrine here!
Where is Pygmalion?

MYR.   Oh, wretched girl!
Art thou not satisfied with all the ill
Thy heedlessness has worked, that thou art come
To gaze upon thy victim's misery?
Well, thou hast come in time!

GAL.   What dost thou mean?

MYR. Why this is what I mean—he will not live
Now that Cynisca has deserted him.
O, girl, his blood will be upon thy head!

GAL. Pygmalion will not live! Pygmalion die!
And I, alas, the miserable cause,
Oh, what is to be done?

MYR.   I do not know.
And yet there is one chance, but one alone;
I'll see Cynisca, and prevail on her
To meet Pygmalion but once again.   [not live

GAL. (*wildly.*) But should she come too late? He may
Till she returns.   [to thee,

MYR. (*as struck by a sudden thought.*) I'll send him now
And tell him that his wife awaits him here.
He'll take thee for Cynisca; when he speaks
Answer thou him as if thou wast his wife.

GAL. Yes, yes, I understand.

MYR.   Then I'll begone,   [2 D. L.
The gods assist thee in this artifice! (*Exit* MYRINE,

GAL. The gods will help me, for the gods are good. [thee,
(*Kneels* o.) Oh, heaven, in this great grief I turn to
Teach me to speak to him, as, ere I lived,

Cynisca spake to him. Oh, let my voice
Be to Pygmalion as Cynisca's voice,
And he will live—for her and not for me—
Yet he will live. I am the fountain head.

Enter PYGMALION, 2 D. L., *unobserved, led in by* MYRINE.

Of all the horrors that surround him now,
And it is fit that I should suffer this;
Grant this, my first appeal—I do not ask
Pygmalion's love; I ask Pygmalion's life.

> (PYGMALION *utters an exclamation of joy. She
> rushes to him and seizes his hand.*)

Pygmalion!

PYG.   I have no words in which
To tell the joy with which I heard that prayer.
Oh, take me to thine arms, my dearly loved!
And teach me once again how much I risked
In risking such a heaven-sent love as thine.

GAL. (*believing that he refers to her.*) Pygmalion! my
    love! Pygmalion!
Once more those words! again! say them again!
Tell me that thou forgivest me the ill
That I unwittingly have worked on thee!

PYG. Forgive *thee?* Why, my wife, I did not dare
To asy *thy* pardon, and thou askest mine.
The compact with thy mistress Artemis
Gave thee a heaven-sent right to punish me,
I've learnt to take whate'er the gods may send.

> (GALATEA, *at first delighted, learns in the course of
> this speech that* PYGMALION *takes her for* CYNIS-
> CA, *and expresses extreme horror.*)

GAL. (*with an effort.*) But then, this woman, Galatea—
PYG.   Well?
GAL. Thy love for her is dead?
PYG.   I had no love.
GAL. Thou had'st no love?
PYG.   No love. At first, in truth,
In mad amazement at the miracle
That crowned my handiwork, and brought to life
The fair creation of my sculptor's skill,

I yielded to her god-sent influence,
For I had worshipped her before she lived
Because she called Cynisca's face to me;
But when she lived—that love died—word by word.

GAL. That is well said; thou dost not love her then?
She is no more to thee than senseless stone?

PYG. Speak not of her, Cynisca, for I swear

Enter CYNISCA U. E. R. *unobserved.*

The unhewn marble of Pentelicus
Hath charms for me, which she, in all her glow
Of womanly perfection, could not match.

GAL. I'm very glad to hear that this is so.
Thou art forgiven! (*kisses his forehead.*)

PYG.   Thou hast pardoned me,
And though the law of Artemis declared
Thy pardon should restore to me the light
Thine anger took away, I would be blind,
I would not have mine eyes lest they should rest
On her who caused me all this bitterness!

GAL. Indeed, Pygmalion—'twere better thus—
If thou could'st look on Galatea now,
Thy love for her, perchance, might come again.

PYG. No, no.

GAL.   They say that she endureth pains
That mock the power of words.

PYG.   It should be so.

GAL. Hast thou no pity for her? (CYNISCA *comes down.*)

PYG.   No, not I.
The ill that she hath worked on thee—on me—
And on Myrine—surely were enough
To make us curse the hour that gave her life.
She is not fit to live upon this world!

GAL. (*bitterly.*) Upon this worthy world, thou sayest well.
The woman shall be seen of thee no more.

(*Takes* CYNISCA's *hand and leads her to* PYG.)

What would'st thou with her now? Thou hast thy
wife!

(*She substitutes* CYNISCA *in her place, and retires,*
U. E. R., *weeping.* CYNISCA *takes him to her arms
and kisses him. He recovers his sight.*)

PYG. Cynisca! see! the light of day is mine!
Once more I look upon thy well loved face!

Enter MYRINE *and* LEUCIPPE, U. E. R.

LEUC. Pygmalion! Thou hast thine eyes again!
Come—this is happiness indeed!
PYG.   And thou?
Myrine has recalled thee?
LEUC.   No, I came,
But more in sorrow than in penitence;
For I've a hardened and a blood-stained heart,
I thought she would denounce me to the law,
But time, I found, had worked a wondrous change;
The very girl, who half-a-day ago
Had cursed me for a ruthless murderer,
Not only pardoned me my infamy, ·
But absolutely hugged me with delight,
When she, with hungry and unpitying eyes,
Beheld my victim---at the kitchen fire!
The little cannibal!

Enter GALATEA, U. E. R., *down* C.

MYR. (*after a pause.*) Pygmalion!
See—Galatea's here! (GALATEA *kneels to* PYG-
MALION).
PYG.   Away from me,
Woman or statue! Thou the only blight
That ever fell upon my love—begone,
      (*She covers her eyes,* CYNISCA *comforts her.*)
For thou hast been the curse of all who fell
Within the compass of thy waywardness!
CYN. No, no—recall those words, Pygmalion,
Thou knowest not all.
GAL. (*rising and backing up stage.*) Nay—let me go
from him;
That curse—his curse still ringing in mine ears,
For life is bitterer to me than death.
        (*She mounts the steps of pedestal.*)
Farewell, Pygmalion—I am not fit

To live upon this world—this worthy world.
> (*Curtains begin to close slowly around* GALATEA.)
Farewell, Pygmalion.   Farewell—farewell!
> (*The curtains conceal her.*)

CYN. (*angrily.*) Thou art unjust to her as I to thee!
Hers was the voice that pardoned thee—not mine.
I knew no pity till she taught it me.
I heard the words she spoke, and little thought
That they would find an echo in my heart;
But so it was.   I took them for mine own,
And asking for thy pardon, pardoned thee!

PYG. (*amazed.*) Cynisca!   Is this so?

CYN.   In truth it is?

GAL. (*behind curtain.*)   Farewell, Pygmalion! Farewell
  —farewell!

> PYGMALION *rushes to the veil and tears it away
> discovering* GALATEA *as a statue on the pedestal,
> as in Act I.*)

[SOFT MUSIC.—SLOW CURTAIN.

THE END.

A MODERN ANANIAS,
Comedy in Three Acts
BY
JOHN A. FRASER, Jr.

Four male, four female characters. Two interior, one exterior scenes. Modern society cotumes. Plays two and one half hours. This is a screaming farcial comedy, which depends upon the wit and humor of its lines no less than upon the drollery and absurdity of its situations for the shrieks of laughter it invariably provokes. Unlike most farcical comedies, "A Modern Ananias" has an ingeniously complicated plot, which maintains a keen dramatic interest untill the fall of the last curtain. The scenery, if necessary, may be reduced to a garden scene and an interior. Every character in the piece is full of comedy of the most humorous description, and one of them, a fat old maid, may be performed by a male somewhat after the fashion of "Charley's Aunt." The climaxes are hilariously funny, and each of the three acts is punctuated with laughs from beginning to end. Amateurs will find nothing more satisfactory in the whole range of the comic drama than this up-to-date comedy-farce by J. A. Fraser, Jr. The fullest stage directions accompany the book, including all the "crosses" and positions, pictures, etc. Price, 25 cents.

'TWIXT LOVE AND MONEY,
Comedy Drama in Four Acts
BY
JOHN A. FRASER, Jr.

Eight male, three female characters. Plays two and one-half hours. Three interior scenes. Costumes of the day. This charming domestic comedy drama of the present day bids fair to rival, both with professionals and amateurs, the success of "Hazel Kirke." The scene is laid in a little village on the coast of Maine, and the action is replete with dramatic situations which "play themselves." The story is intensely interesting and, in these days of Frenchy adaptations and "problem" plays, delightfully pure; while the moral—that love brings more happiness than does money—is plainly pointed without a single line of preaching. No such romatic interest has been built up around a simple country heroines since the production of "Hazel Kirke" and "May Blossom" years ago. The play is in four acts, and as the scenery is easy to manage it is particularly well adapted for the use of amateurs. There are three female parts, two of them comic characters, and eight males, two of whom supply the comedy. The dressing is all modern and the piece forms a full evening's entertainment. The author, J. A. Fraser, Jr., has been highly successful as a dramatist for the professional stage, having written. "The Noble Outcast" "Edelweiss." "The Merry Cobbler." The Train Wreckers," "A Delicate Question." "A Modern Ananias." "Becky Bliss, the Circus Girl," and many other well-known and successful plays. "Twixt Love and Money" has been carefully revised by the author for the amateur stage. Price 25 cents.

The Dramatic Publishing Company, Chicago.

THE MERRY COBBLER.
Comedy Drama in Four Acts
BY
JOHN A. FRASER, Jr.

Six male, five female characters. Two interior, two exterior scenes. Modern costumes. Time of play, one hour and forty-five minutes. This refined, yet laughter-making comedy, in which John R. Compson starred successfully for several seasons, has been carefully revised by the author for the amateur stage. This romantic story of a German imigrant boy in New Orleans, who falls in love with, and finally marries, a dashing Southern belle, is one of the cleanest and daintiest in the whole repertoire of the minor stage. In addition to the Merry Cobbler himself, who is one of the type the late J. K. Emmet so loved to portray, there are five other male characters, five female parts and very short parts for two little girls. Had the piece been originally written for the use of amateurs, it could not have been happier in its results, its natural and mirth-provoking comedy combined with a strong undercurrent of heart-interest, rendering it a vehicle with which even inexperienced actors are sure to be seen at their best. The scenic effects are of the simplest description and the climaxes, while possessing the requisite amount of "thrill" are very easy to handle. This piece has been seen in all the larger cities of the Union during the past four seasons, and is now placed within the reach of amateurs for the first time. J. A. Fraser, Jr., author of "The Merry Cobbler," and a score of other successful plays, has prepared elaborate instructions for its production by amateur players. Price, 25 cents.

A DELICATE QUESTION,
Comedy Drama in Four Acts
BY
JOHN A. FRASER, Jr.

Nine male, three female characters. One exterior, two interior scenes. Modern costumes. Plays two hours. If a play presenting an accurate picture of life in the rural districts is required, in which every character has been faithfully studied from life, nothing better for the use of amateurs than "A Delicate Question" can be recommended. The story is utterly unlike that of any other play and deals with the saloon, which it handles without gloves and at the same time without a single line of sermonizing. What "Ten Nights in a Barroom" was to the public of a past generation, "A Delicate Question" is destined to be to the present, although it is far from being exactly what is known as a "temperance play." The plot is intensely interesting, the pathetic scenes full of beauty, because they are mental photographs from nature, and the comedy is simply uproariously funny. The parts, very equally balanced. The scenic effects are quite simple, and by a little ingenuity the entire piece may be played in a kitchen scene. The climaxes are all as novel as they are effective and the dialogue is as natural as if the characters were all real people. The author, J. A. Fraser. Jr., considers this one of his greatest successes. Price, 25 cents.

The Dramatic Publishing Company, Chicago.